D0538755

COP 22

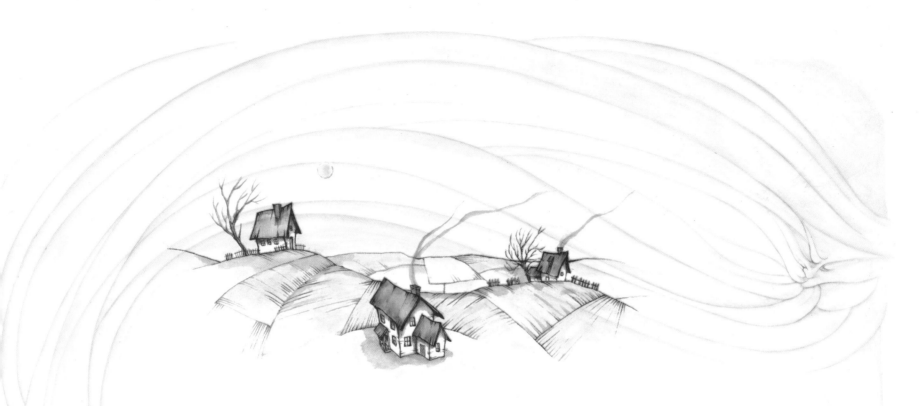

Little Pieces of the West Wind

STORY BY CHRISTIAN GARRISON

PICTURES BY DIANE GOODE

BRADBURY PRESS   SCARSDALE, NEW YORK

The text of this book was set in 18 pt. Aldine Bembo. The illustrations were preseparated by the artist for four-color reproduction. Ms. Goode painted the black and white base plate on parchment and the three overlays on acetate using a fine brush and black China ink.

FOR *A. W.G.* FOR *David*

—C. G. —D. G.

Once there was a clever old man who
had lost his socks.

"I know a way to get back my socks,"
said the clever old man to himself.

He opened his door and all of the windows
and then sat down to wait for the West Wind.

That afternoon the West Wind came
blustering through the open door and windows
of the cabin.

Just as the West Wind entered,
the clever old man jumped up, slammed shut
the door, and closed all of the windows
with a bang.

"Ha!" he said to the West Wind.
"I have caught you!"

Sure enough. The wild West Wind blew
and bounced about inside the cabin, but was unable
to get away.

"What do you want of me, old man?"
bellowed the West Wind.

"I have lost my socks, and I want you
to find them for me," said the clever old man.

"I am the wild and reckless West Wind!
I work for no man!" wailed the West Wind.

He swelled and blew and crashed against
the window, but could not find so much
as a tiny crack to seep through.

The clever old man chuckled, and the
West Wind finally agreed to do as he asked.
"But I do not trust you, West Wind.
So I will keep a little piece of you here with me
until you return with my socks."
    With that, the clever old man pulled off
a piece of the West Wind and wrapped it in a rug.
Then he opened the window, and what
was left of the mighty West Wind blew away
to look for the clever old man's socks.

Soon the West Wind came upon a woodchopper
who was wearing socks on his hands.
  "You make a funny sight with socks
on your *hands*," said the West Wind with a whistle.
  "Who cares?" grunted the woodchopper
without looking up.
  "Where are your gloves?" asked the West Wind.
  "Lost," grumbled the woodchopper.
  "Let me have those socks!" hissed the
West Wind.
  "No," said the woodchopper, "not unless
you find my gloves."

The West Wind sputtered and howled.
At last he agreed to do as the woodchopper asked.
"But I do not trust you, West Wind.
So I will keep a little piece of you here with me
until you return with my gloves."
    With that, the woodchopper chopped off
a piece of the West Wind and put it inside
a hollow log and stopped up the hole,
and what was left of the mighty West Wind
blew through the trees to look
for the woodchopper's gloves.

Soon the West Wind came upon a gypsy
who was wearing a pair of gloves on her head.
"You make a funny sight with gloves
on your *head*," wailed the West Wind.
"Goodness me! Do I?" giggled the gypsy,
blushing from head to toe.
"Have you no scarf?" the West Wind asked.
"I cannot find it anywhere," said she.
"I would like to have those gloves,"
said the West Wind.
"I should say not, you silly wind!"
snapped the gypsy. "But if you bring me back
my scarf, then you may have these gloves."

The West Wind shook the trees and rustled
the leaves, but finally agreed to do as she asked.
"But I do not trust you, West Wind.
So I will keep a little piece of you here with me
until you return with my scarf."

With that, the gypsy pinched off a piece
of the West Wind and placed it inside her tea tin
where she kept her tea leaves, and what was left
of the once mighty West Wind wandered away
to look for the gypsy's scarf.

Soon the West Wind came upon a sheep
who had a scarf around his leg.
 "You make a funny sight with that scarf
around your *leg,*" wheezed the West Wind.
 "BAAAAA!" cried the sheep.
 "Why are you wearing that scarf?"
the West Wind asked.
 "Because I have lost my blue ribbon
I won at the fair," sobbed the sheep.
 "Give me the scarf, sheep," said the West Wind.
 "NOOOOO!" said the sheep. "Go find
my blue ribbon, and then I shall gladly
give you this scarf."

The West Wind was too tired by now
to fuss and fume, and he agreed to do as
the sheep asked.
"But I do not trust you, West Wind.
So I will keep a little piece of you here with me
until you return with my blue ribbon."
With that, the sheep bit off a piece
of the West Wind and stuffed it under his
haystack to keep. And what was left of
the once mighty West Wind floated off
to look for the sheep's blue ribbon.

Soon the West Wind came upon a bird
who had a blue ribbon in her tail.
 "You make a funny sight with that
blue ribbon in your *tail*," whispered the West Wind.
 "You would too!" chirped the bird.
 "Have you lost your tail feather?"
the West Wind asked.
 "Yes indeed!" sang she.
 "May I please have that blue ribbon, bird?"
whined the West Wind.
 "You may not!" said the bird. "Find my
tail feather, and you may have this blue ribbon."

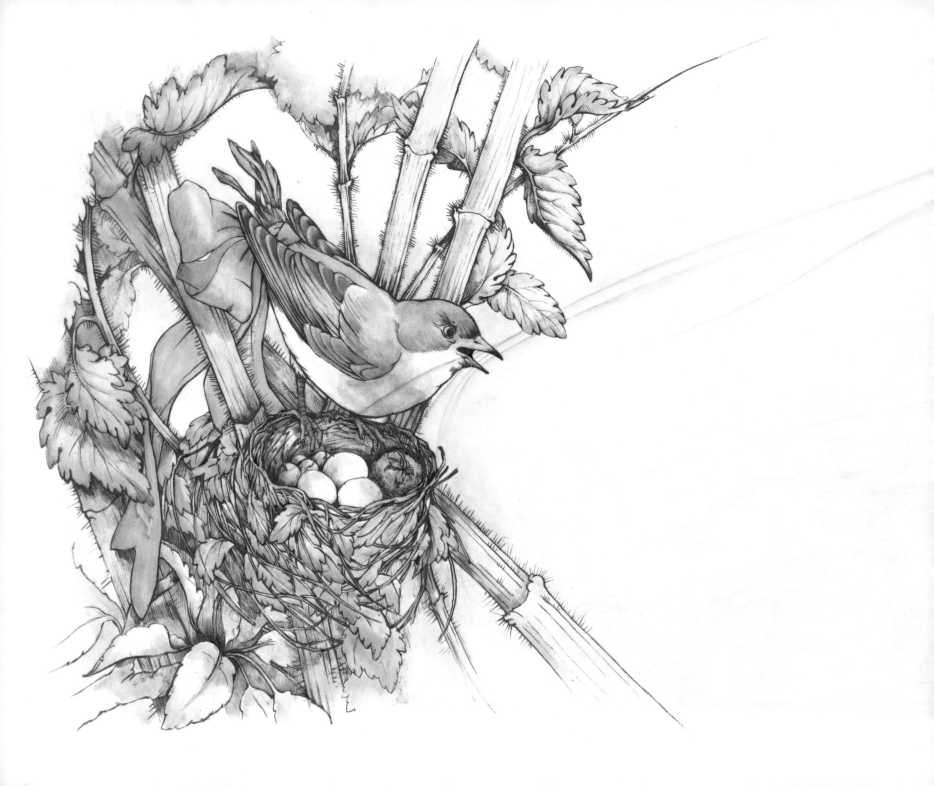

All the West Wind could do was sigh
and agree to do as the bird asked.
 "But I do not trust you, West Wind.
So I will keep a little piece of you here with me
until you return with my tail feather."

    With that, the bird pecked off a piece
of the West Wind and stuck it under her nest
to keep.

    By now the West Wind was nothing more
than a puff of breeze as he went to look
for the bird's tail feather.

At last the West Wind came upon a
little girl who was playing with a feather.
  "Please give me your feather, young lady,"
sighed the West Wind.
  "I can barely hear you. Why do you whisper,
and who are you?" the little girl asked.
  "The mighty West Wind," said he.
  "Why, you are nothing more than a tiny puff
of breeze," she replied.
  "That is because others have pulled,
chopped, pinched, bitten, and pecked away
little pieces of me," the West Wind whispered.
  "I will give you this feather, West Wind.
But will you come back to see me every afternoon
to cool me off and keep me company?"

He was too weak to refuse. So the
tiny puff of breeze that once was the mighty
West Wind took the feather and went away
to keep all of the bargains he had made that day.
   The bird got back her tail feather
and returned the blue ribbon
and the little piece of wind.

The sheep got back his blue ribbon
and returned the scarf
and the little piece of wind.

The woodchopper got back his gloves
and returned the pair of socks
and the little piece of wind.

The gypsy got back her scarf
and returned the pair of gloves
and the little piece of wind.

The West Wind was growing mighty
and strong again by the time
he arrived at the cabin of the clever old man.
"Come out, old man! I have returned
with your socks, and I want the piece of me
you are keeping!"

Gladly the clever old man unwrapped
the rug and let out the piece of wind
he was keeping there.

And that made the West Wind whole again.

The clever old man chuckled
and sat down to put on his socks
as the mighty West Wind blustered away.